ER
VIRJA N
FOREST PARK PUBLIC LI
W9-BYA-815
What this story needs is a munch and a
32026002770151

FOREST PARK PUBLIC LIBRARY

BAKER & TAYLOR

What This Story Needs Is a Munch and a Crunch
Copyright © 2016 by Emma J. Virján. All rights reserved. Manufactured in China. No part of this book may be used or reproduced in any manner whatsoever without written permission except in the case of brief quotations embodied in critical articles and reviews. For information address HarperCollins Children's Books, a division of HarperCollins Publishers, 195 Broadway, New York, NY 10007. www.harpercollinschildrens.com

Library of Congress Control Number: 2015947624
ISBN 978-0-06-241529-5

The artist used charcoal sketches painted digitally to create the illustrations for this book.
Typography by Dana Fritts
16 17 18 19 20 SCP 10 9 8 7 6 5 4 3 2 1
❖ First Edition

WHAT THIS STORY NEEDS IS A MUNCH AND A CRUNCH

By Emma J. Virján

FOREST PARK PUBLIC LIBRARY
JUL -- 2016
FOREST PARK, IL

HARPER
An Imprint of HarperCollins*Publishers*

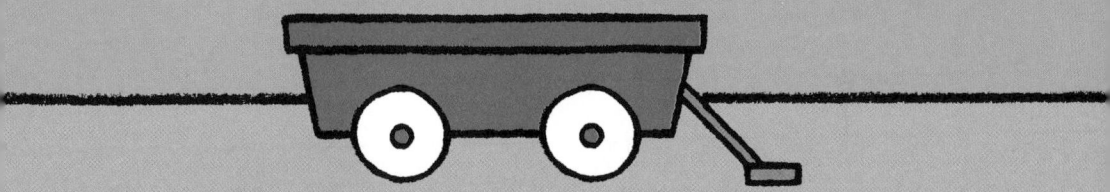

What this story needs is
a pig in a wig,

baking bread,

pouring punch,

and meeting a friend
for a picnic lunch.

This story also needs
a blanket,

some plates,

a few carrots

and pies,

some sandwiches,

apples,

ketchup and fries,

a game of catch,

a kite in the breeze,

and good friends
munching and crunching
by the trees.

Whoosh
Boom
Plop
Splash

What this story needs now
is a mad dash!

Quick!
Grab the blanket,
plates, carrots,
and pies,

the sandwiches,
apples, ketchup
and fries.

What this story needs now is . . .

another place to eat.

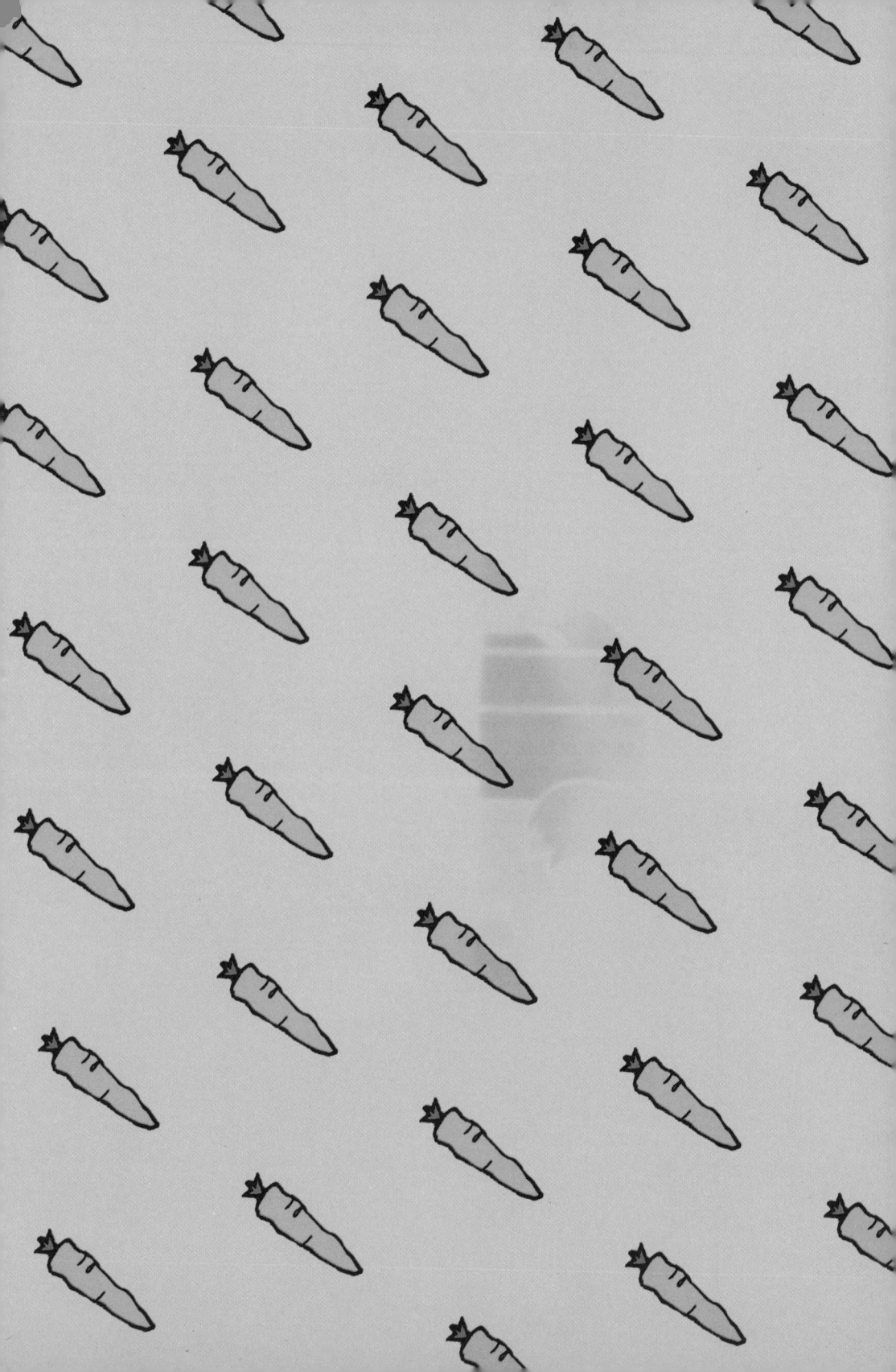